Will Princess Isabel Ever Say Please?

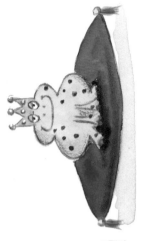

by STEVE METZGER

illustrated by AMANDA HALEY

Holiday House / New York

To Annie Scavo and Robbie Farkas

—S. M.

To my best friend and sister, Melissa

—A. H.

Library of Congress Cataloging-in-Publication Data

Metzger, Steve.
Will Princess Isabel ever say please? / by Steve Metzger ;
illustrated by Amanda Haley. — 1st ed.
p. cm.
Summary: Princess Isabel has such bad manners that even though she has many
chances to marry a handsome prince, each one is put off by her rudeness.
ISBN 978-0-8234-2323-1 (hardcover)
[1. Princesses—Fiction. 2. Etiquette—Fiction. 3. Fairy tales.]
I. Haley, Amanda, ill. II. Title.
PZ7.M5675Wi 2012
[E]—dc22
2010048168

From the top of her tiara to the tips of her petite feet, Princess Isabel was perfect in every way but one: she wouldn't say "please."

One day a prince, wanting to find a bride, held a ball to which every princess was invited.

The prince liked Isabel best of all.

Bopping and stomping and jigging and jogging, Isabel lost track of time.

When the clock struck midnight, which was when she told her stepmother she'd be home, she dashed away, leaving one dainty slipper behind.

Slipper in hand, the prince traveled far and wide in search of the small-footed princess.

He found her at last. But just as Princess Isabel was about to place her tiny toes into the elegant shoe, the prince stopped.

"Say 'please,'" said the prince.

"No," said Isabel.

Declaring "You are too rude to be queen of my realm," the prince left the shoe and Isabel too.

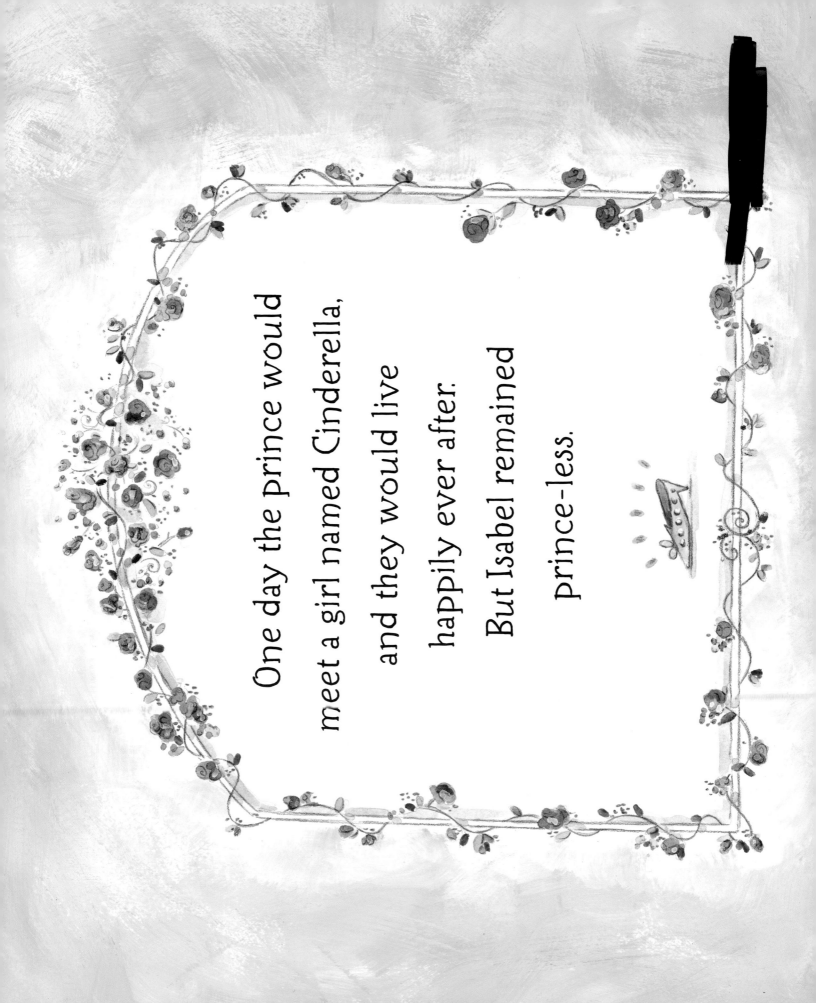

One day the prince would meet a girl named Cinderella, and they would live happily ever after. But Isabel remained prince-less.

Time passed. Princess Isabel grew prettier and prettier. She was even more beautiful than her stepmother, the queen.

Every morning the beautiful queen asked her mirror who was fairest in the land. She was, of course. But one day the mirror said . . .

Thou, Queen, art fair and beauteous to see. But Princess Isabel is lovelier than thee!

Green with envy, the queen told her huntsman to take Princess Isabel out into the scary, dark forest and kill her.

"That takes care of that," said the queen, happy to be fairest once again.

But she was not, as her mirror would explain. . . .

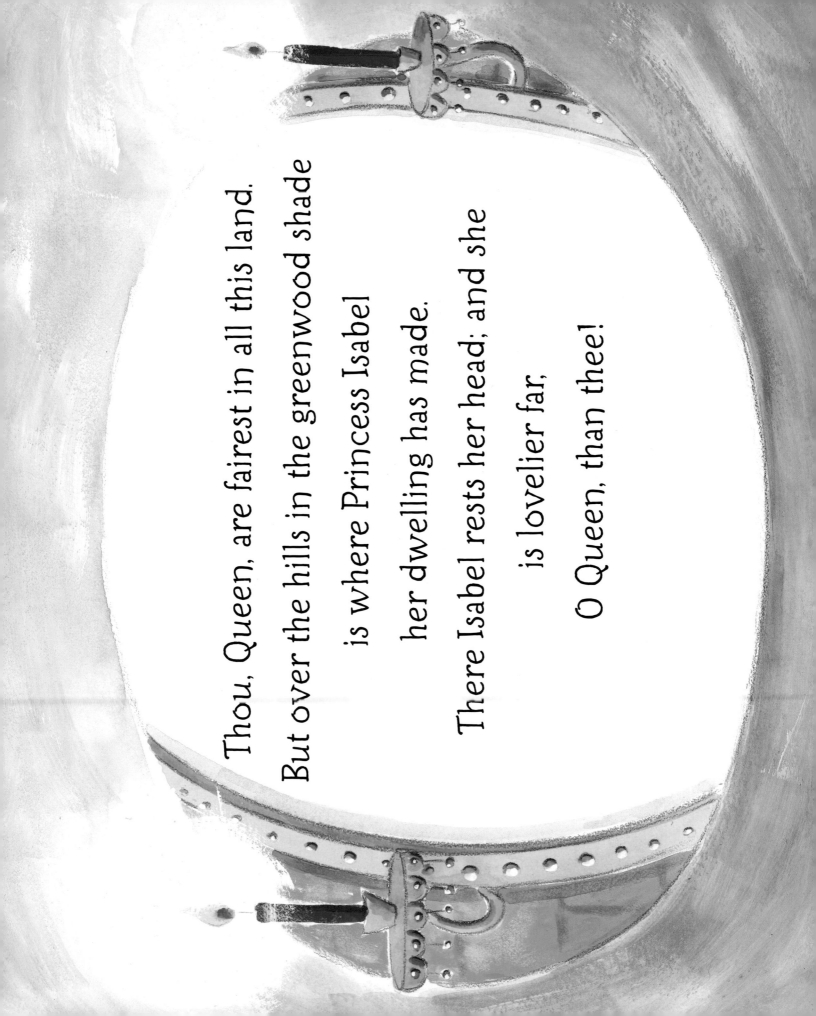

Thou, Queen, are fairest in all this land.
But over the hills in the greenwood shade
is where Princess Isabel
her dwelling has made.
There Isabel rests her head; and she
is lovelier far,
O Queen, than thee!

The queen was furious.
"If you want a job done right, do it yourself!" she said.
Disguising herself as a poor old woman with a strong resemblance to Groucho Marx and taking a poison apple with her, she set out for the house in the greenwood shade . . .

. . . where she startled Princess Isabel, who had, indeed, indeed, been resting her head.

Isabel saw the apple and grabbed for it. But the queen held it back. "No," said the queen. "You did not say 'please.' You may be pretty, but you have no manners. You are no threat to my beauty."

One day a girl named Snow White would be poisoned by an apple, fall into a deep sleep, and be awakened by a prince.

But not Isabel.

She remained prince-less.

One morning Princess Isabel was tossing her favorite golden ball when it fell into a spring so deep that she could not see the bottom.

Princess Isabel wailed.

"What ails you, king's daughter?" said a talking frog that happened along.

"I lost my ball," the princess said. "Get it for me, and I will give you pearls and jewels and even my golden crown."

"I don't want pearls or jewels or your golden crown," said the frog. "I'll get your ball if you just say 'please.'"

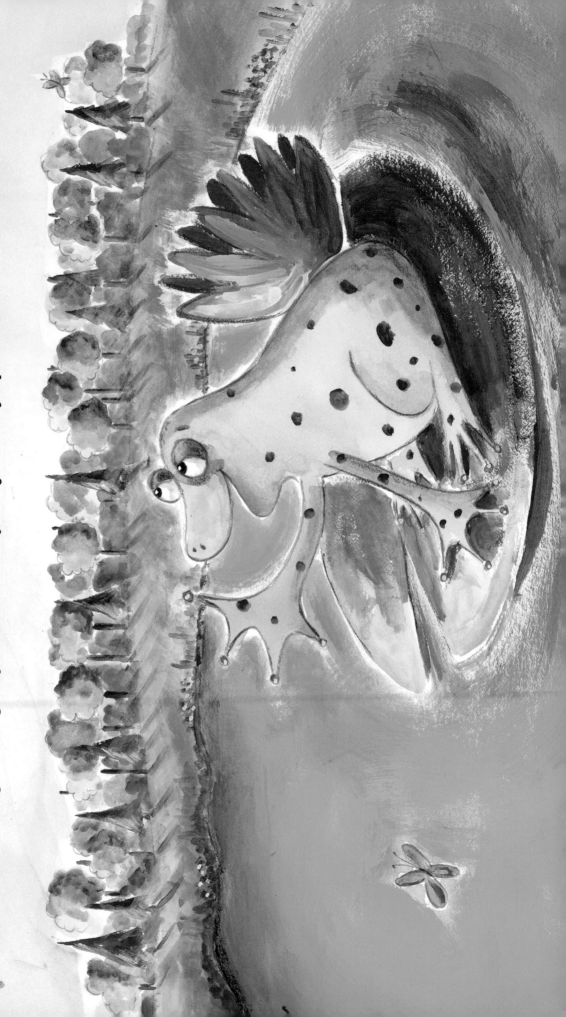

But Princess Isabel wouldn't say please,
and the frog wouldn't get the ball.

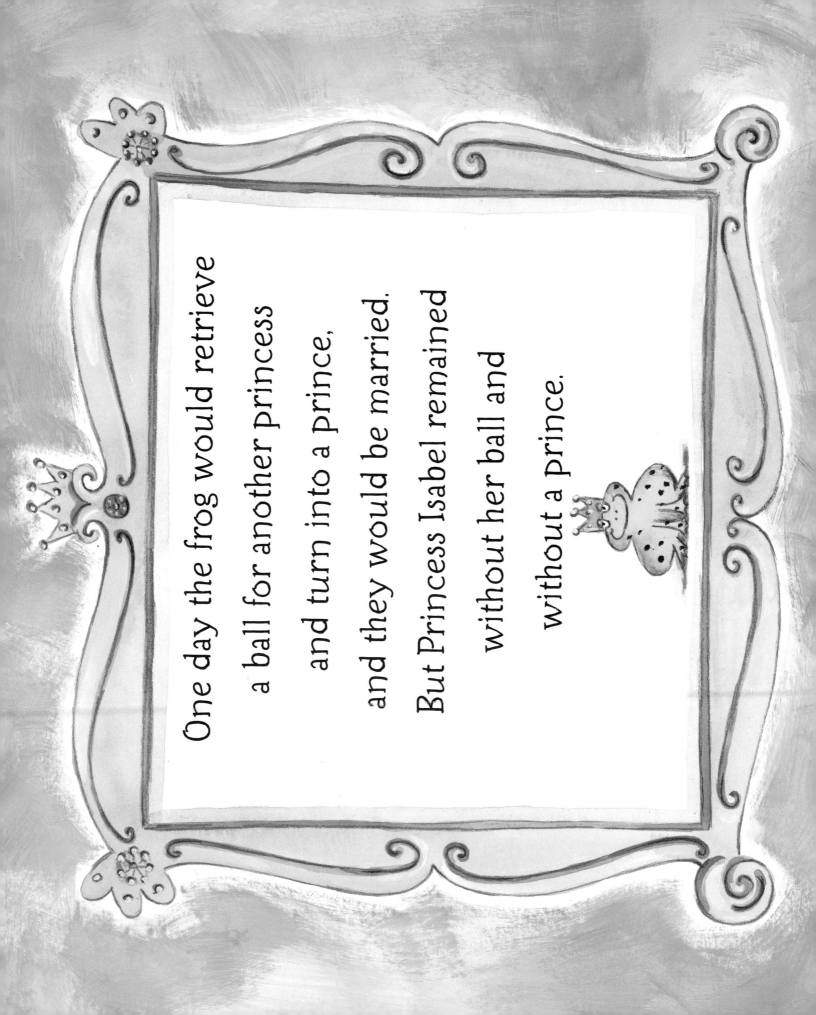

One day the frog would retrieve
a ball for another princess
and turn into a prince,
and they would be married.
But Princess Isabel remained
without her ball and
without a prince.

One afternoon while strolling in a forest, Princess Isabel realized she was lost. "HELP!!!!!!!" she cried.

Just then a gallant prince rode by on his horse.
"Why do you cry?" asked the prince.
"I'm lost," Isabel sobbed. "Will you help me?"

And then an amazing idea came to her. "Will you help me, *please*?" When the prince heard Princess Isabel say "please," he was so impressed by her humility and fine manners that he fell in love with her on the spot.

"Will you marry me?" he asked.
"Oh, yes!" she replied. "Yes, if you please."

Princess Isabel finally found her prince. And she was very pleased!